In Search of the Perfect Pumpkin

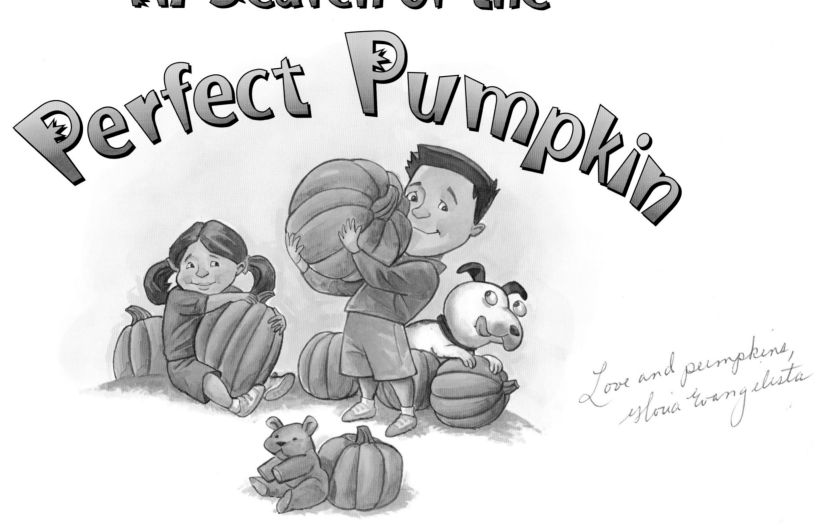

*Love and pumpkins,
Gloria Evangelista*

Gloria Evangelista • Illustrated by Shawn Shea

Fulcrum Resources
Golden, Colorado

**Dedicated to Michael, Josh and Zach
for eating all those pies**

Library of Congress Cataloging-in-Publication Data

Evangelista, Gloria.
  In search of the perfect pumpkin / Gloria Evangelista ; illustrated by Shawn Shea.
    p. cm.
  ISBN 1-55591-994-4
  1. Pumpkin—Juvenile literature. 2. Cookery (Pumpkin)—Juvenile literature. [1. Pumpkin. 2. Cookery—Pumpkin.] I. Shea, Shawn, ill. II. Title.
  SB347 .E93 2001
  635'.62—dc21   2001001698

Printed in Singapore
0 9 8 7 6 5 4 3 2 1

Fulcrum Publishing
16100 Table Mountain Parkway, Suite 300
Golden, Colorado 80403
(800) 992-2908 • (303) 277-1623
www.fulcrum-resources.com

I was as high as a baseball bat, skinny as one too, when Mom decided to bake fresh pumpkin pies for fall, and so we went in search of the perfect pumpkin.

What are the world's largest fruits? Pumpkins. The largest ones can weigh over 1,000 pounds!

We purchased our pumpkins at the local grocery store the first year. A sign read, "Sugar Pumpkins! Great for Baking!"

I asked the produce man, "How great are these pumpkins? Are they, 'Hooray, the Giants won again!' great, or are they, 'Due to the weather, all schools will be closed until further notice,' great?"

I definitely preferred the second.

He said, "Don't know. Never baked with sugar pumpkins before."

How to pick a perfect pumpkin: make sure it is firm all over, but especially firm on the bottom.

We took our chances and bought the pumpkins because we were chance-taking kind of people, the kind who rode in the front seat of the Killer Cyclops or meandered through the woods with slithering rattlesnakes and screeching coyotes.

Pumpkins were once recommended for removing freckles and curing snakebites.

The sugar pumpkins made good pies, not "Giants-winning," "school-closing" kind of pies, but everyone liked them. Even my dog, Chromium Picolinate, seemed pleased when my sister shared a piece with him, although Mom wasn't too happy.

Pumpkin pie was not eaten at the Thanksgiving feast, nor for that matter was anything sweet. What supply of sugar the Pilgrims brought on the *Mayflower* had dwindled by the time of the feast. Also, Pilgrims did not have ovens.

The next year we drove to a pumpkin patch in search of the perfect pumpkin. A scarecrow right out of *The Wizard of Oz* pointed to an entire mound of them with a sign that read, **"UNBELIEVABLE PIE PUMPKINS."**

In early colonial America, pumpkins were used as an ingredient for the crust of pies, not the filling.

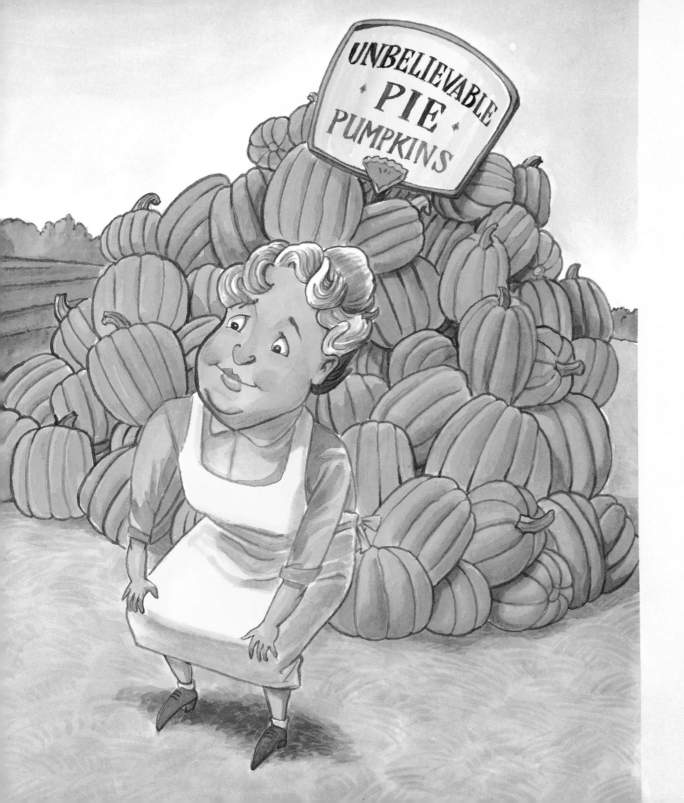

I asked, "How unbelievable are these pumpkins? Are they, 'Our turtle lived in the vacuum cleaner for an entire month and is still alive,' unbelievable, or are they, 'You just won $500 worth of merchandise from the toy store—shop till you drop,' unbelievable?"

I hoped it was the second.

"These pumpkins are truly unbelievable," the lady said. "They were grown in the rich valleys of Iowa, picked fresh, and hauled here."

The only thing I found unbelievable was the fact that Iowa was far away and her truck looked as if it couldn't make it around the corner. I snooped around for a Batmobile. However, Mom felt if the pumpkins were good enough for Dorothy and Toto, they were good enough for us.

The pumpkins from Iowa made good pies, not "Your turtle lived in a vacuum cleaner," "Go raid the toy store" kind of pies, but everyone liked them.

Even my sister refused to share, although I'm not sure if it was because she liked the pie so much or was just tired of scrubbing it off the floor.

Pumpkins have been food sources, symbols, and even toys for longer than recorded history.

The next year, we went organic. I was just glad we weren't going to Iowa. We drove to a farm where all the fruits and vegetables are grown without the use of chemical sprays or pesticides. Those are things that farmers use to keep pests like bugs and rabbits away.

I wondered if they worked on sisters.

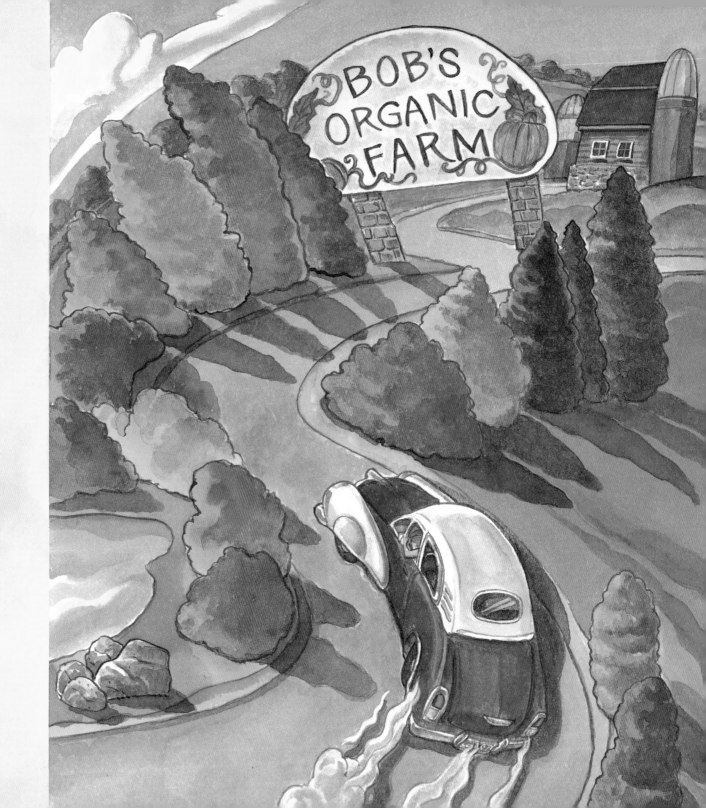

"You want Sugar Babies," the man said. "They're scrumptious for baking."

"How scrumptious are they?" I asked. "Are they 'gooey cheese pizza right out of the oven when I'm starving' scrumptious? Or are they 'melt in your mouth, drippy chocolate and marshmallow s'mores, gotta have another piece' kind of scrumptious?"

Either one of those would be fine with me.

One pumpkin plant will normally produce 3 to 5 pumpkins, sometimes more. Miniature varieties will produce one dozen or so.

He said, "They're 'You'd better buy them now because I'm not picking any more until Thanksgiving' scrumptious."

We knew a good thing when we saw it.

Pumpkins have been grown in America for over 5,000 years and were completely unknown in Europe before the time of Columbus.

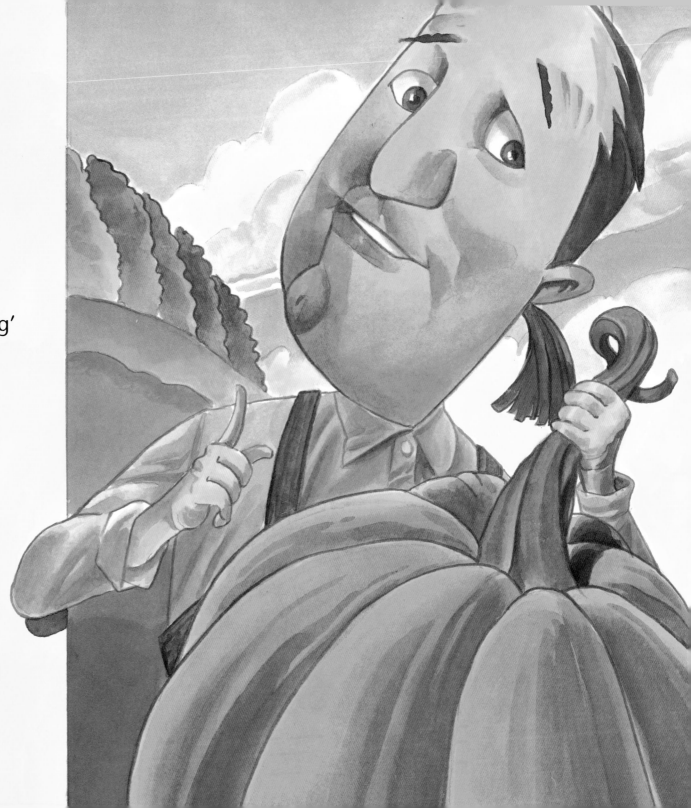

The organic Sugar Babies pumpkins made good pies, not "gooey cheese pizza right out of the oven" pies or "melt in your mouth, gotta have another piece" kind of pies, but everyone liked them.

The Native Americans of the eastern United States considered pumpkin almost as important a food as corn and beans. Pumpkins were baked or boiled, and the seeds were ground into meal for gruel or bread.

Thus another year passed and we remained in search of the perfect pumpkin. Finally Mom announced, "This year we will grow our own pumpkins."

Dad said they will be the greatest, most unbelievably scrumptious pumpkins of all, and Dad knew everything, like if you walk barefoot on the moon you will get sticky marshmallow feet and to never attempt to climb Mount Everest if you eat only cookies for breakfast.

The single most important factor in determining where to locate a pumpkin patch, is to make sure it gets lots of sun.

And so our garden began.
We planted,
we watered,
we weeded,
we hoed,
Took but a week for those
seeds to explode.
We covered,
we fertilized,
we prayed for
no snow.

Tips: Soak seeds in warm water for an hour or two before planting. Plant the seeds 1 inch deep, pointed end down. That's where the root will come out.

Leaves sprawled in the yard, they sprawled in the road.

Soon a green vine grew to a bright yellow flower. A bulb followed that … and then a ball, then I hollered. …

The flowers of pumpkins are edible.

Do chirping birds and crickets help plants grow? Yes! Scientists have found that certain sounds cause pores in plant leaves to open, resulting in stronger growth.

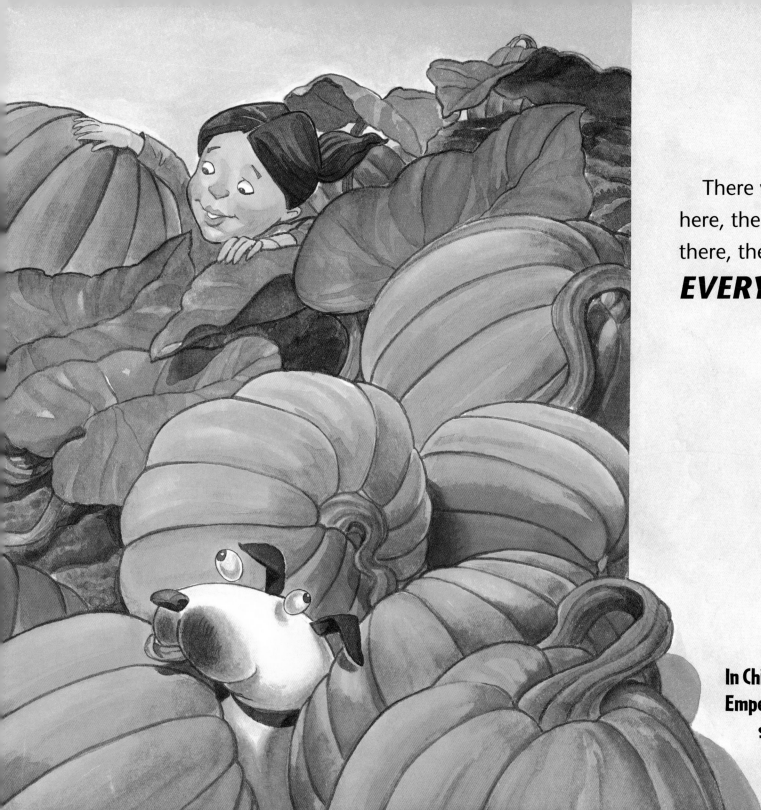

There were pumpkins here, there were pumpkins there, there were pumpkins **EVERYWHERE!**

In China, the pumpkin is the Emperor of the Garden, symbol of fruitfulness, health, and reward.

We named them …

Portabello,
  Monticello,
    Sneakers, and Sublime,
Mammaletti,
  Somba-getti,
    Tweekers, and Past Prime
There was Dollarwise and
  Penny Foolish
    News at Five and
      Hammer Tool-Dish.

One pumpkin plant produced 2,715 pounds of pumpkin. It was grown from a seed won in a raffle. The plant produced four pumpkins weighing 774, 686, 652 and 603 pounds. All were healthy.

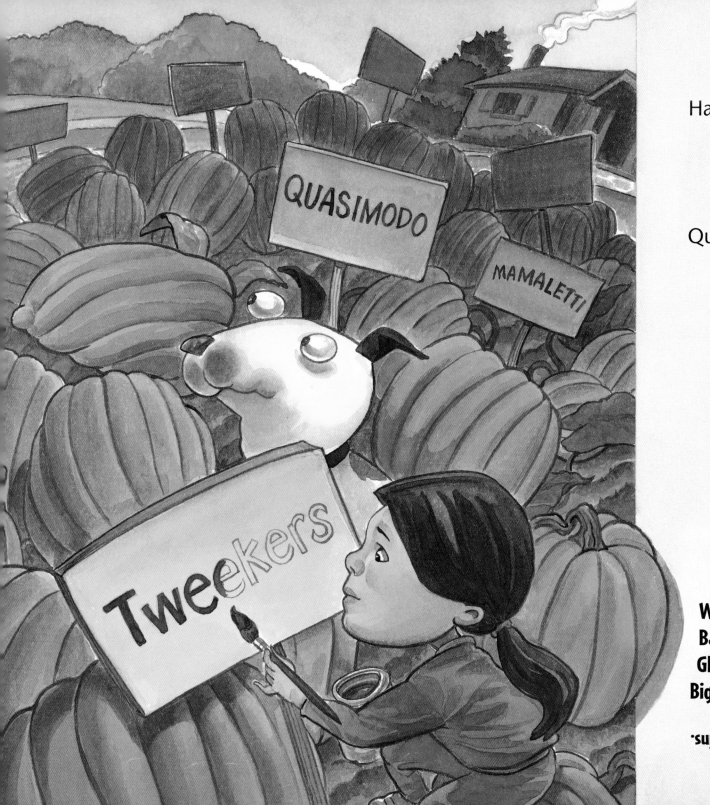

Hackety Sackety and
Pumpernickel
smelled like melon,
looked like pickle.
Quasimodo and
Toto too
sprawled around
this pumpkin zoo.

**What do the names Munchkin,
Baby Boo, Jackpot, Frosty,
Ghost Rider, Jumpin' Jack,
Big Max, and Gremlin describe?**

All are different varieties of pumpkins.

We picked them,
    we washed them,
        we seeded,
            we baked,
we made pies,
    we made breads,
        we made
            orange fruitcake.

And do you know what?

**A 4-pound pumpkin yields about
4 cups of mashed pumpkin meat.
Two cups make one pie.**

Our pumpkins made the greatest, most unbelievably scrumptious, "Giants-winning," "school-closing," "turtle alive in the vacuum cleaner," "raid the toy store," "gooey cheese pizza right out of the oven," "melt in your mouth s'mores" kind of pies … anyone ever tasted.

Make horns from the hollow stems of pumpkins. Cut off the stalk. The cut end will be hollow. Scrape off prickles, then put in your mouth and blow. Big stalks make a mooing sound that may actually call cows.

From The Kitchen Of....

THE PERFECT PUMPKIN PIE

2 cups of fresh pumpkin (slightly chunky)
2/3 cup of sugar
1/2 tsp. salt
3 and 1/4 tsp. of pumpkin pie spice
3 slightly beaten eggs
6-ounce can of evaporated milk
5/8 cup non-fat milk (can use regular, if preferred)
1 9-inch unbaked pastry shell, preferably deep dish

For a deep dish pie, you will need approximately one pumpkin per pie. Cut pumpkin in half and place face down in a baking dish in about an inch of water. Bake at 350 until soft. Do not overcook. Remove the seeds and peeling. Mash pumpkin in bowl until slightly chunky, not whipped.

Combine pumpkin, sugar, salt, and spices. Blend in eggs, milk, and evaporated milk. Pour mixture into pastry shell (crimp edges high as amount is generous). Cover edges of crust with foil until a few minutes before pie is done, then remove to brown.

Bake in hot oven (400) for about 45 minutes or until inserted knife comes out clean. Cool. Place pecan halves on top to decorate, if desired. Serve with vanilla ice cream and a dollop of whipped cream. Enjoy.